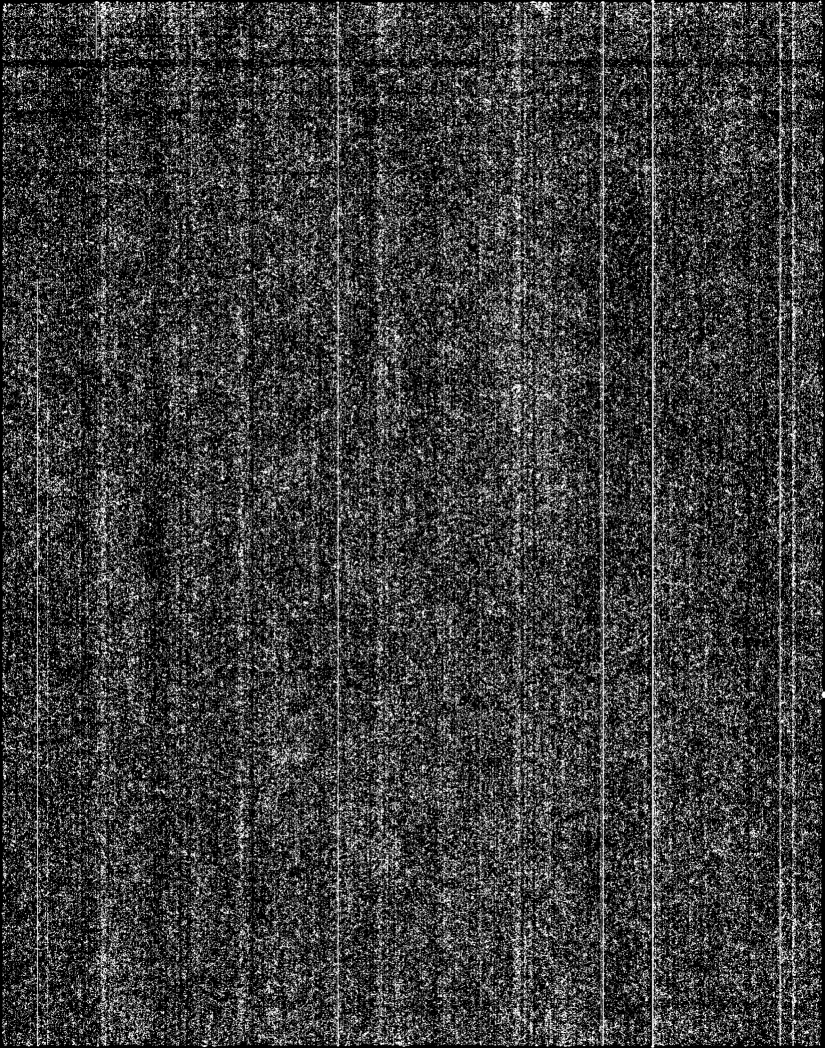

Disney
Christopher Robin

A Boy, a Bear, A BALLOON

By Brittany RUBIANO • Illustrated by Mike WALL

For Matthew: Christopher Robin says it best:
"You are braver than you believe, stronger than you seem,
and smarter than you think." —BR

For Thiago: Born during the making of this book. —MW

Printed in the United States of America
First Hardcover Edition, July 2018
10 9 8 7 6 5 4 3 2 1
ISBN 978-1-368-02588-1
FAC-034274-18138
Library of Congress Control Number: 2017959435
Designed by Gegham Vardanyan
For more Disney Press fun, visit www.disneybooks.com

DISNEP PRESS
Los Angeles • New York

LONG AGO, THERE WAS A BOY NAMED
CHRISTOPHER ROBIN, who had many friends in the
Hundred-Acre Wood. It was a wondrous place filled with tea
parties, adventures, and games. Time passed by, as time is
wont to do, and the boy grew up. He spent years and years
away from his friends. But one friend in particular, a bear
with a hankering for honey, knew Christopher Robin would
return. And return he did.

ONE BLUSTERY DAY, the Hundred-Acre Wood had a very special visitor– none other than Christopher Robin. . . . AN OLDER, **BIGGER** Christopher Robin.

Winnie the Pooh was delighted to have his old friend back.
Even if he was a bit frownier than Pooh
remembered, and spoke of strange things like

"RESPONS-

BIL-A-BEES."

Christopher Robin thought the Hundred-Acre Wood seemed different, too. "Pooh, was it always this gloomy?" he asked, gripping his case of Important Things. "We don't seem to be getting anywhere."

"Normally," Pooh mused, "I just wait for SOMEWHERE to come to me. We could stop until this mist is . . . mistless."

But Christopher Robin decided he could get them unlost.

They trudged on and soon came
across an alarming warning.

"Oh, bother," said Pooh.

"There are no such things as
Heffalumps and Woozles," said
Christopher Robin.

"Of course there are," Pooh replied.
"Didn't you see the sign?"

Luckily, the pair didn't meet any
Heffalumps or Woozles . . .
or even any Jagulars. But they
did come across some familiar
tracks.

"Those are our footsteps!"
Christopher Robin cried.
"We just went in a circle!"

Just then, Christopher Robin's case of Important Things flew open. Sheets of paper twirled through the sky. "**NOOOO!**" he exclaimed.

Pooh offered his balloon, for no one could be un-cheered with a balloon.

Yet Christopher Robin was still not cheered. "There's more to life than balloons and honey!" he yelled. "I'm not a child. I'm an adult now!"

"But you're Christopher Robin," Pooh said.

"No," Christopher Robin replied. "I'm not how you remember me."

With that, Christopher Robin hurried to gather his Important Things.
When he was done, he realized a certain bear was gone.

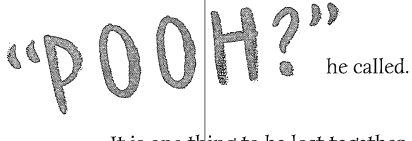

"POOH?" he called.

It is one thing to be lost together. It is quite
another to be lost apart. So Christopher Robin
searched high and low for his friend until . . .

ROO

WARNING

HEFFALUMP
and WOOZLE

OOOAAARRRRR!

A loud Heffalump-y sound cut
through the Wood.

Heffalumps and Woozles are not real,
Christopher Robin reminded himself.

In fact, Christopher Robin was so busy NOT looking for Heffalumps,
he fell right into a Heffalump trap.

♪ AND DOOOOOWN, DOOOOWN HE WENT.

It seemed Christopher Robin was stuck.

He was not sure how the day could get any worse. Then it began to rain.

"POOH? ANYONE? HELP!"

Christopher Robin yelled and tried to climb and yelled some more.

HEFFALUMP TRAP
GOTCHA!

But he could not get unstuck. After a while, Christopher Robin tuckered himself out so much he fell asleep.

"Sometimes the thing to do is NOTHING,"
Dream Pooh told him.

"Nothing?" Christopher Robin frowned.

"Yes," Dream Pooh answered. "It often leads to the best
SOMETHING."

When he awoke, Christopher Robin found the Heffalump trap was almost filled with water. He started to panic. Then he remembered Dream Pooh's Very Good Advice.

"JUST DO NOTHING."

And wouldn't you know, Christopher Robin floated to the top, making his way out of the Heffalump trap.

Muddier, if a little gladder, Christopher
Robin went to find Pooh and the rest
of his friends. Soon he spotted
none other than his
old pal Eeyore.

"Just my luck," the donkey said. "A Heffalump, leering at his lunch."

Christopher Robin shook his head.

"EEYORE, I'M NOT A HEFFALUMP!"

"Doesn't matter anyway. Headed for the waterfall. Be gone soon," Eeyore replied.

"Oh! Don't worry, Eeyore," Christopher Robin called. "I'll save you!"
Throwing his hat and case and coat to the ground, he dove into the river.

It wasn't as deep as it once was.

"Right," Christopher Robin said as he stood up.
"I'm grown now." He let out

A BIG BOOMING LAUGH

—the first one he'd had in years.

"Laughing at my misfortune," Eeyore observed. "Oh, well."

Reminded of the task at hand, Christopher Robin quickly
grabbed the donkey and got him safely to shore.

"Hello, Heffalump," Eeyore said
once they were out of the river.

Christopher Robin helped him dry off. "I'm not a Heffalump, I'm
Christopher Robin, the one who used to try and cheer you up."

Eeyore stared at him. "I don't remember being cheery."

Christopher Robin decided to move on to a different topic. "How did
you end up in the water?" he asked.

"Woke up. Windy. House blew down. Fell in the river.
Can't swim—"

ROOOOOOOAAAARRRRR!

A loud Heffalump growl interrupted them.

Christopher Robin and Eeyore decided to look for the others.

When they got to Owl's house, they discovered it
had fallen down, just like Eeyore's. The blustery
day had clearly been one of the Wood's
blusteriest.

ROOOOOOOOAAARRRRR!

Another Heffalump call sounded. *Heffalumps are not real,*
Christopher Robin thought again.

Summoning all his courage, he crept closer and closer to the
house, only to find . . .

"Aha!" There was the noisy culprit:
a broken weather vane on Owl's roof.
Christopher Robin laughed.
Of course!

RRROOOOAAA~

Christopher Robin stopped
the "Heffalump" mid-roar.

"But no Owl . . ." he observed.
"What happened?"

Christopher Robin peered
through a hole in Owl's roof.
"They were all here. I see Rabbit's
carrots . . ." He felt the uneven
roof planks. "And someone
was bouncing—Tigger."

PLEZ CNOKE IF
AN RNSR IS
NOT REQID

PLEZ
RING IF
AN RNSR
IS REQID

Christopher Robin then
spotted another clue. "Haycorn
shells—a whole trail of them!"

"Follow them and we'll find
Piglet," Eeyore said.

Christopher Robin and Eeyore
hurried through the Wood,
from one haycorn to the next,
calling out for their friends.

After a little while, they heard a
squeaky voice: "Who is it? Who's
th-th-there?"

"It's just me," Eeyore replied.

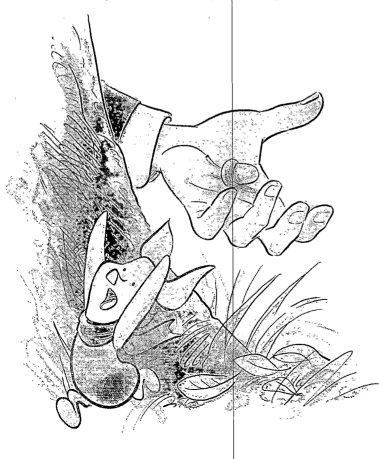

Little Piglet breathed a sigh of
relief as he stepped out from behind
a tree. "Eeyore, thank goodness
it's you."

"OH, AND A HEFFALUMP."

Eeyore nodded toward
Christopher Robin.

Piglet screamed, running off, despite
Christopher Robin's protests.

They followed Piglet to a large hollow log.

"Piglet, you've led the Heffalump right to us!" Rabbit's voice reprimanded.

"Hello, everyone!" Christopher Robin called. Suddenly, a blur of black and orange stripes bounced in front of him.

"I'LL POUNCE YA, I'LL POUND YA—"

"Tigger, it's Christopher Robin!" Christopher Robin said.

Eeyore sighed. It was time to find out once and for all. He peered at Christopher Robin. And wouldn't you know . . .

"It is," Eeyore decided.

"YOU CAN SEE IT IN HIS EYES NOW."

Christopher Robin's grin spread from the bottoms of his feet to the top of his head.

"Well, how about that?" Tigger cheered. "Our old pal!"

"Ah, yes, I see it," Owl said. "Never really doubted it at all.
Would you like to join us, Christopher Robin? We're hiding
from the Heffalump."

"But the Heffalump was just your old weather vane, Owl," Christopher Robin told him.

Rabbit's long ears twitched. "Oh, dear, he's addled in the brain. Happens to the elderly."

"Poor old thing," Kanga added.

"The beast is real," Tigger explained to Christopher Robin. "We heard it this morning."

"And worse, Pooh has gone missing," Owl said.

Christopher Robin suddenly felt a rumbly in his tumbly that he knew had nothing to do with hunger.

Roo peeked out of Kanga's pouch. "I'm not leaving until it's gone for good."

Piglet joined him. "Me—me neither."

"There's no such thing as monsters," Christopher Robin explained.

But then Christopher Robin saw the looks on their faces—faces of old, dear friends he hadn't seen in a very long time. They needed his help.

He decided, in this case, NOTHING would not do.
He would have to do SOMETHING.

"You're right, Roo," he declared. "We've got a scary Heffalump here, and it's time I defeated it!"

And so, Christopher Robin and Eeyore set off once more, now on
a hunt for a beastie.

"Aha! There it is," Christopher Robin said, pointing
in the direction of a large clearing.

"STOP, HEFFALUMP!"

"This is complete silliness," he whispered as he put his coat and necktie to good use.

"You gonna beat the Heffalump or not?" Eeyore asked.

Christopher Robin nodded, mustering all of his old Christopher Robin-ness.

"HEFFALUMP, I'LL TEACH YOU TO SCARE MY FRIENDS!"

He took a breath, and he whacked the silly
Heffalump with all his might.

He ducked and dodged, leaped and lunged.

"AH!" "NO!" "ROAR!" "TAKE THAT!"

The Heffalump put up a good fight, and Christopher Robin found he was enjoying himself and doing well . . . aside from one tactical error.

Eeyore looked behind him. "There goes the tail. Typical."

The others listened intently from the log, cheering on their hero.
Then all went quiet.

"Did the Heffalump beat him, Mommy?" Roo asked.

"Well, Christopher Robin is very old now, deary," Kanga replied.

Suddenly, Christopher Robin came into view. "Victory is ours!" he announced, beaming.

"HIP-HIP-HOORAY!" THEY CRIED. "HIP-HI

The friends gathered round to celebrate. But Christopher Robin knew there was one Very Important Bear missing. The only trouble was . . . Christopher Robin still didn't know where to find him. The grown-up boy had looked all the places Pooh wasn't, and none of the places Pooh was.

"You're Christopher Robin," Roo said encouragingly. "You'll find him somewhere."

Christopher Robin suddenly got a Very Good Idea. He clapped his hands. "That's it, Roo! He's waiting for Somewhere to come to him!"

And so Christopher Robin led the way to

SOMEWHERE.

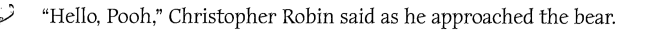

"Hello, Pooh," Christopher Robin said as he approached the bear.

"Hello, Christopher Robin." Pooh Bear smiled. The balloon bobbed, and Christopher Robin waved at Pooh.

He tried to find the right words. "I'm so terribly sorry, Pooh. I never should have yelled."

"But I am a bear of very little brain," Pooh replied.

Christopher Robin sat beside him. "YOU ARE, I THINK, A BEAR OF VERY BIG HEART."

The friends hugged. Christopher Robin told Pooh about the Heffalump, about helping the others, and about how he had been feeling lost for quite some time.

"But I found you, didn't I?" Pooh asked.

So he had. Really, they had found each other. . . .

AND SOMEWHERE WAS A VERY GOOD PLACE TO BE, INDEED.